THE
QUEEN'S NECKLACE
A SWEDISH FOLKTALE

RETOLD BY JANE LANGTON

ILLUSTRATED BY ILSE PLUME

HYPERION BOOKS FOR CHILDREN
NEW YORK

Text © 1994 Jane Langton.
Illustrations © 1994 Ilse Plume.
Based on a literary fairy tale,
Drottningens Halsband (The Queen's Necklace)
by Helena Nyblom (1843–1926).
Translated by Tommy Olof Elder, 1992.
First Edition
1   3   5   7   9   10   8   6   4   2

Library of Congress Cataloging-in-Publication Data

Langton, Jane
The Queen's Necklace: a Swedish folktale/retold by Jane
Langton; illustrated and designed by Ilse Pume; [translated by Tommy Olof
Elder] — 1st ed.
p.   cm.
"Based on a literary fairy tale, Drottningens halsband ('The
queen's necklace') by Helena Nyblom" — T.p. verso.
Summary: A cruel and greedy king prizes a pearl necklace above
all, but the kindhearted young woman who becomes his wife gives the
pearls away one by one to help the poor.
ISBN 0-7868-0011-9 (trade) — ISBN 0-7868-2007-1 (lib. bdg.)
[1. Fairy tales.   2. Sweden — Fiction.]   I. Plume, Ilse, ill.
II. Nyblom, Helena, 1843–1926. Drottningens halsband.   III. Title.
PZ8.L28St   1994
[E] — dc20   93-34817   CIP   AC

*"If a book comes from the heart,
it will contrive to reach other hearts"*
— CARLYLE

THE QUEEN'S NECKLACE

A SWEDISH FOLKTALE

ing Hendrik was a bad king.

If his horse stumbled, he ordered his men to kill it and bring him another.

If beggars came to his castle, he whistled for his dogs, and they growled at the beggars and chased them away.

If his dinner was cold, he threw the cook into one of the dark dungeons beneath the great banqueting hall.

He was cruel, too, to the people of his kingdom. He taxed the farmers heavily for the harvests of their fields, and the fishermen for the eels they caught in the river. He taxed the merchants for the pots and pans they sold to the housewives, and the blacksmiths for the nails and hinges they hammered, red-hot from the blazing hearth.

So the people grew poorer and poorer, and the king richer and richer. Greedily he built new palaces and filled them with furniture studded with jewels.

But his most precious possession was a necklace.

It was a beautiful necklace, a string of one hundred pearls. Ninety-nine were perfect — large and round and glowing with light. Only the hundredth pearl was small and uneven.

With all his wealth, his palaces and his pearls, King Hendrik still felt poor. There was no one to love him. He had no wife or children, no mother or father. His younger brother was dead. Only his nephew was left, Prince Nils.

One day the king commanded Nils to go out into the countryside and find him a wife. "She must be beautiful, of course," said the king, "and perfect in every way, worthy of my necklace of perfect pearls."

"Perfect?" laughed Nils. "No one is perfect. Even your string of pearls isn't perfect. One of the pearls is uneven and smaller than the rest. But I will try, Uncle, to find you a wife."

Mounting his horse, Nils set forth, riding through the countryside, visiting one poor village after another. Often the people he met on the road were thin and hungry and cold. They clung to his bridle and cried, "Help us!"

Soon Nils had given away his cloak, his gloves, and his saddlebags filled with food. He found many pretty girls, but none of them was perfect. One had a big nose, another was too thin, a third was rude and bad-tempered. Still another laughed in his face when he told her King Hendrik was looking for a wife. "I have seen the king," she said scornfully. "He is old and mean and ugly. Who would want to marry him? Not I."

But one day as Prince Nils rode past a ramshackle farm deep in the country, he saw a young girl looking over a fence into a barnyard. She was lovelier than any girl he had ever seen before, and she was laughing. His heart went out to her.

Dismounting, he went to the girl and said, "Why are you laughing, mistress?"

"I'm laughing at the new little pigs," she said. "Look at the way they tumble over each other! And there are fluffy new chicks in the hen coop, and the lambs are skipping in the field. And look at the way the clouds are playing in the sky."

"What is your name, mistress?"

"Blanzeflor. It means White Flower."

Nils was delighted. Not only was Blanzeflor beautiful, she had a warm and joyous heart. Surely she was perfect in every way. "May I speak to your father, Blanzeflor?"

At once she led him into the barn, where he found an old man milking a cow. The cow was thin and scrawny, and only a little milk dribbled into the pail.

Her father's name was Pontus. He looked up with astonishment at the splendid young prince. "What do you want of me, great lord?"

"Good sir," said Nils, "King Hendrik is looking for a wife. Will you permit your daughter to be his queen?"

At the same moment, the cow fell to her knees, too weak to stand, and old Pontus rose from the milking stool. He looked at his daughter gravely. "It is up to you, my daughter. I have heard that the king is old and ugly. We know that he has a hard heart."

Blanzeflor looked solemnly back at him. "The cow is too starved to give milk. The last of the sheep must soon be sold, and the sow and her litter. Yes, Father, I will marry the king. He will not let the father of the queen go hungry. Do not worry about me. The sun will shine over his castle as brightly as it shines here, the clouds will race across the same blue sky, the trees will spread the same leafy shade, the cocks will crow in the morning. I will find happiness in these things, Father, just as I do now."

Sorrowfully the old man embraced Blanzeflor and turned away with bowed head.

Nils, too, had an aching heart. Pitying poor Blanzeflor, he set her high on his horse. Then, taking the bridle in his hand, he led her over hill and dale, through all the hungry villages, back to the castle of King Hendrik.

Of course the king was overjoyed by the success of his nephew's mission. "Ah, Nils," he said, gloating over the beauty of his bride, "you have done well. She is indeed as perfect as my string of pearls."

Blanzeflor shuddered, and lowered her eyes. Humbly, she stood still while the king's seamstress fitted her with a magnificent bridal gown.

The wedding in the royal church was stately and majestic. Nils watched silently as the bishop raised his hands and declared Hendrik and Blanzeflor to be man and wife. With all his heart Nils wished that he had never found the beautiful laughing girl named Blanzeflor. Surely she would never laugh again as the wife of King Hendrik.

Sadly Nils looked on as the king fastened the string of pearls around his new wife's neck. It seemed to Nils that they shone with a greater radiance than before, a glow arising from Blanzeflor's own pure heart.

But the king scowled at his new bride. "You must wear them always," he warned her. "The day I find you without them will be your last."

Thus began Blanzeflor's queenly life. Nils had been right. Her days were filled with sorrow. She saw all her husband's cruelties as he filled the prisons with starving people who had stolen crusts of bread and raised the taxes higher still, to pay for the new castle he was building for his bride.

"I don't need a new castle," said the queen. "I am perfectly content with this one."

Poor Blanzeflor! As the wife of the wicked king she had only two pleasures. One was the quiet devotion of Prince Nils. The other was her joy in the birds of the air. Within the castle walls everything was made of stone and gold and heavy ornament, and the courtiers powdered their faces chalk-white and covered their heads with towering wigs of horsehair. But when Blanzeflor looked out the window of her bedchamber, she saw the blue sky and the trees of the forest and the birds, and it made her glad.

Every morning at dawn she rose from her bed and went to the open window to scatter crumbs on the sill. Winter had come, the snow was deep, the days were bitter cold. The hungry birds came fluttering to her, squeaking like scissors, murmuring like water pouring from a jug, chattering like children. The house sparrow, the jay, and the chaffinch came to her window, along with the blue tit and the snow bunting — chuckling, warbling, whistling, pecking at the crumbs on the windowsill.

"Oh, little birds, you make me laugh," said Blanzeflor. Smiling, she came out of her chamber to tell Prince Nils that the birds gave her joy.

Nils was glad to see her smile, but he knew she hid her sorrow in her heart.

One night there was a strange noise in her bedchamber. Blanzeflor was awakened by a small sound, a little thump on the floor.

She sat up in bed. By the light of the stars she saw a small stone on the embroidered carpet. Someone had tied a note to the stone and thrown it through the open window.

Blanzeflor lit a candle and read the note.

Queen Blanzeflor takes pity on the birds of the air!
Will she pity, too, the people of the earth? I am a poor
widow in the village to the west. My six children have
only one coat. While one is warm, the others shiver.
Help us!

Blanzeflor went to the window and looked out, but she could see no one. The poor widow was gone.

At once the queen's heart beat with gentle pity, and she wept for the widow and her children. Taking off her necklace, she held it in her hands and looked at the hundred shining pearls. "One pearl will make no difference," she said to herself. "My husband will never notice it is gone."

12

In the morning she called Nils to her side. Removing a single pearl from the necklace, she put it in his hand. "Quickly," she said, "take this to the village to the west and give it to the widow with six children."

Nils was eager to serve her. At once he took the pearl and rode to the village west of the king's palace. In a tumbledown cottage he found the poor widow with all her children huddled around her knees. Only the youngest wore a coat. The others trembled in rags.

"Take this," said Nils, handing the pearl to the widowed mother. "It is a gift from Queen Blanzeflor."

The poor woman wept with gratitude. "The queen is a pearl among women," she sobbed, and kissed his hand.

That evening the queen came down to dinner in the banqueting hall, just as usual, and sat beside the king. Her necklace shimmered in the candlelight. No one noticed that one of the pearls was missing.

But that night another letter came thumping through her window, wrapped around a stone. It came from a fisherman in the village to the east.

The king's bailiffs claim that the eels in the river are royal property. They have forbidden us to catch them. How are we to live?

Again the queen wept with pity. Once more she pulled a pearl from her necklace. This time she told Nils to take it to the poor fisherman.

He rode away at once and presented the queen's gift. "Ah!" cried the fisherman, "Queen Blanzeflor is a pearl among women."

The next night another stone crashed to the floor of the queen's bedroom with a message from the bishop of the royal church.

His Majesty has robbed the altar of its splendor. Now we must worship God with candlesticks of lead and a chalice of tin!

In the morning Blanzeflor pulled a third pearl from her necklace and told Nils to carry it to the bishop.

"God bless the good queen," exclaimed the bishop, falling to his knees. "She is indeed a pearl among women."

And every night thereafter a poor sufferer beseeched the queen for help. Again and again the queen pulled loose another pearl from her necklace and sent Nils to bring it to someone in need.

Nils did her bidding willingly. But one day he warned her, "Dear Queen, you have taken away half the pearls from your necklace. Surely the king will notice they are gone."

"No," laughed the queen, "he will notice nothing. Look!" Pulling the ribbon from her long braid, she let her hair fall down her back, so that it hid the empty part of the string of pearls.

But the errands of mercy went on and on. Every day there were fewer pearls around Blanzeflor's neck. Soon the hair hanging down her back could no longer conceal the missing pearls. Cleverly she pulled it forward so that it hung over her shoulders. Still the king noticed nothing.

But her generosity did not stop. Every morning for ninety-nine days Blanzeflor pulled another pearl from the necklace to help her people — to warm their shivering limbs and dry their tears and feed their hunger.

At last not a single pearl was left. Even the small imperfect pearl was gone.

Nils feared for Blanzeflor's life. "Oh, my queen, what will you do now? The king will see that the string of pearls is empty!"

"Oh no," said Blanzeflor, smiling, and she crossed her hair under her chin like a scarf and pinned it with a rose as white as her name.

But the king was not to be fooled. When Blanzeflor entered the banqueting hall he stared at her and said peevishly, "All I can see is the tip of your nose." Roughly he tore away the rose. At once Blanzeflor's hair fell back and revealed her bare throat.

The king turned red with rage. Like an angry peacock he screamed at her, "Where is my string of pearls?"

"Oh," said the queen, "I took it off because it didn't match my gown." Carelessly she laughed as if she had forgotten the king's dread command that she must never remove the necklace on pain of death. Only Nils could see the trembling of her sleeves.

"Send for them," thundered the king. "Send for the pearls!"

Shrugging her shoulders, Blanzeflor sent her maid to look for the necklace in her bedchamber.

The maid found nothing. She came back wringing her hands, and knelt before the queen. "I am sorry, Your Majesty, I cannot find them."

At once the king sprang to his feet. His chair fell back with a crash. Leaning over Blanzeflor, his face crimson with rage, he roared at her, "Where are they? What have you done with my pearls? To whom did you give them? Tell me his name, and he will hang from the topmost tower!"

Blanzeflor said nothing. She could not betray the good people to whom she had given the pearls. She sat silent as the king stamped up and down in his fury. "Go, all of you!" he bellowed to the lords and ladies of his court. "Go, search everywhere! Find my pearls!"

Away they all went, scurrying timidly, rushing into every corner of the castle, every nook and cranny, trying to find the missing string of pearls. They tore the blankets from the beds, threw open the chests and hampers, ransacked the wardrobes, and searched in each other's pockets. Nils went with them, pretending to look with the rest.

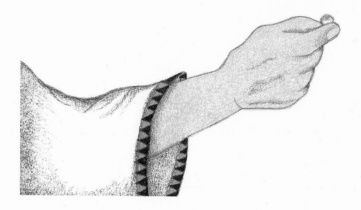

All came back empty-handed—all but one.

It was the king's own manservant, sly Torsten. Running to the king in triumph, he held out his hand. Between his fingers was the little imperfect pearl.

The king's eyes bulged. "Where did you find it?" he whispered. His voice was hoarse from shrieking.

"Under your nephew's pillow," said sly Torsten, grinning.

"My nephew!" croaked the king. In his wild fury he ordered his armed men to drag Nils forward. "You traitor!" he bellowed at Nils. "Where are the rest of my pearls?"

Nils said nothing. He only wished that he had given away the very last pearl as well.

But—foolish Nils!—he had kept it as a token of his love for Blanzeflor.

He blamed himself for his mistake. The queen was perfect, a pearl among women, and he loved her with all his heart. It was he who was imperfect like the hundredth pearl, the one he had kept for himself.

Blanzeflor's eyes filled with tears as the king ordered Nils cast into prison. "Hang him at dawn," he commanded his soldiers, "from the topmost tower!"

Blanzeflor, too, was dragged off to the dungeon. "We will cut off her head in the morning," sneered the king, grinning at the lords and ladies of his court, who tut-tutted among themselves and flapped their hands. What could they do to save the poor queen? They were helpless. They could do nothing at all.

Nils and Blanzeflor were imprisoned in two of the dark dungeons below the banqueting hall. But each dungeon had a window, and they could talk to each other through the bars.

"It is my fault you are going to die, dear Nils," said Blanzeflor sorrowfully.

"No, it is mine, dear Queen," said Nils, "for saving the last pearl as a keepsake."

Their beds were merely heaps of straw. Nils lay down, but he could not sleep. It was his last night on earth. It was the last night, too, for the queen he loved.

Early next morning he got up and went to the window to see the dawning of his last day. To his surprise flocks of birds were circling overhead, fluttering around the high window of the queen's bedchamber.

Nils called to them softly, "Come, little birds."

At once they flew down to him. "Come in," whispered Nils. "You are small enough to fit between the bars."

Soon all the birds were gathered around him. They perched on his knees, his shoulders, his arms, and he told them of the queen's plight.

The dove crooned in sorrow, "Poor, poor queen."

"She fed us every day," chirped the sparrow.

"In the cold and snow of winter," warbled the wren.

"Never fear," murmured the chaffinch. "We will find a way to save her."

And then the birds crept out between the bars and hovered in the air. Nils could see them coming and going, flying off to the woods and returning. Soon the sky was alive with birds whistling their silvery cries. The air glowed with a pearly light.

22

When the sun rose at last, it sent a single ray into Blanzeflor's narrow dungeon and woke her up. Sadly she went to the window to see the sunrise.

She, too, was surprised when she found the birds gathered on the sill, just as if she were back in her own bedchamber. She smiled at them. "What, my friends—you have found me again? I'm sorry, but this time I have nothing to give you."

But then she stood back in astonishment as the birds flew through the bars of the window. All the birds she had known before were there, and more besides: waxwings and woodpeckers, wrens and bullfinches, magpies and jays, goldcrests and chaffinches, siskins and sparrows. Even a great raven and a shrike squeezed through the bars.

They circled around Blanzeflor's head in a cloud. Dumbfounded, she sank down on the bed of straw. One by one the birds came to her and dropped pearls into her lap.

"This is a tear you wept for the widow with six children," sang the waxwing.

"You wept this tear for the fisherman," chuckled the blue tit.

"This tear was for the schoolmaster," rasped the magpie.

"This, too, is one of your tears," whistled the bullfinch. "You wept it for the bare altar in the church."

Dozens of birds fluttered around her and dropped their pearls until her lap was filled with her own enchanted tears, glowing and shining with alabaster light.

Laughing with joy, Blanzeflor thanked them as they hovered over her and floated about the room, filling it with the hushed whispering of their wings.

24

Then there was a harsher sound: the rattle of the chain on the door as death entered the dungeon. It was the king with three armed men. One wore a black hood and carried an axe. He had come to cut off Blanzeflor's head. Another carried a rope to make a noose for the neck of Prince Nils.

"Farewell, Blanzeflor," said the king, looming over her. "Now you will discover the reward for your treachery."

But when he saw the heap of shining pearls in Blanzeflor's lap, he forgot about cutting off her head; he failed to notice the birds darting around him; he did not hear the croaking of the raven, the screeching of the jay.

"Blanzeflor," he cried, "my pearls! Where have you been keeping them?" At once he began snatching them up in handfuls. They streamed between his fingers and fell on the floor and bounced into corners. "Count them!" he cried to his men. "I expect she is cheating me."

The greedy words were his last. The raven screamed and pecked at the king's head, the jay shrieked and flew at his eyes, and finally the hooked beak of the shrike pierced his heart.

He fell bleeding to the floor. Blanzeflor cried out and knelt beside him, the last pearls tumbling from her lap.

But the king was dead. Gravely she rose to her feet, and at once all the birds began to sing.

The armed men bowed before her. The executioner tore off his black hood and threw down his axe. "You are free, my queen. And so is our new sovereign, King Nils."

"The king is dead!" The cry went through the castle. "Our wicked king is dead! His nephew Nils is king! Long live King Nils!" There was great rejoicing in the castle and in the countryside and in all the cities and villages. Soon there were festivals everywhere in celebration of the marriage of Queen Blanzeflor and King Nils.

Bells rang in the church tower. Birds rollicked in the sky. Even the timid lords and ladies smiled. For years they had been afraid to speak, afraid to laugh or cry, afraid to breathe. Joyfully they danced in the street and threw their powdered wigs in the air, rejoicing in the wedding of the new king and queen.

28

Only the executioner was disappointed. After the wedding he crept back into Blanzeflor's cell, hoping to find the shining pearls that had streamed through the king's fingers and tumbled from Blanzeflor's lap. He meant to seek them out, every last one, and become rich.

He could not discover a single pearl. He found only pools of water. The pearls had turned themselves back into tears, the generous tears shed by the noble queen for the sorrows of her people.

But now she had no need for tears. Once again laughter rose from Blanzeflor's light heart, from her joy in the skipping lambs and the tumbling pigs, the falling snow of winter, the crystal rain of spring, and the summer sun spreading warmth and light all over the land. And before long she laughed with King Nils in wonder at the ten perfect toes of their newborn son, who was called Pontus after his grandfather.

"How perfect he is," they said to each other proudly. "What a perfect little child!"

But whether Prince Pontus would grow up to be a perfect boy and a perfect man, it was far too soon to tell.

About Helena Nyblom

Born in Copenhagen, Denmark, in 1843, Helena Roed married a Swedish professor and writer, Carl Rupert Nyblom, and lived thereafter in Uppsala, Sweden, where her husband taught at the university. Their home was a lively center for artists, musicians, and writers. Carl became well known in Sweden as a writer, a critic, and a poet. His wife, too, was famous for her novels and stories, especially for her literary fairy tales. She died in 1926.

Helena Nyblom was only one of the many women of her time publishing *Kunstmärchen,* romantic fairy stories reflecting the morals and ideals of their writers. In these tales it is hard work that is rewarded, along with helpfulness and love of home. The emotional life of the characters is usually more fully described than in traditional folktales. This literary fairy tale, *Drottningens Halsband (The Queen's Necklace),* illustrates another belief strongly shown in many of these stories, a connection between nature and goodness. The helpfulness of the birds in Blanzeflor's time of trouble is a reward for her kindness to them earlier in the story.

Helena Nyblom was also a strong believer in the importance of independent thought and self-realization for women. Thus she put her own stamp on the story by showing the bold independence of Blanzeflor in disobeying her husband's command about the string of pearls.

I have changed the tale in some ways, replacing Nyblom's nameless squire with Prince Nils, and the accidental death of the wicked king with his destruction by the birds. Above all, I have tried to use the pearls as a metaphor for Blanzeflor herself.

—Jane Langton

37267000201840

E
L

Langton, Jane.

**The Queen's necklace
: a Swedish
folktale.**

**ROBT ERSKINE SCH 88 ERSKINE RD
RINGWOOD, NEW JERSEY 07456**